For Judy and Ellen

Library of Congress Cataloging-in-Publication Data

Yee, Wong Herbert.
EEK! There's a mouse in the house / Wong Herbert Yee.
p. cm.
Summary: After discovery of a mouse in the house, larger and larger animals are sent in after one another, with increasingly chaotic results.
RNF ISBN 0-395-62303-0 PAP ISBN 0-395-72029-X
[1. Animals — Fiction. 2. Stories in rhyme.] I. Title.
PZ8.3Y42 1992
[E] — dc20 91-41823
CIP
AC

Printed in China
LEO 30 29 28 27 26 25 24 23
4500346780

EEK! There's a Mouse in the House

WONG HERBERT YEE

Houghton Mifflin Company • Boston

EEK!

There's a Mouse in the house.

Send in the Cat
to chase that rat!

Uh-oh!

The Cat knocked over a lamp.

Send in the Dog
to catch that scamp!

Dear me!

The Dog has broken a dish.

And now the Cat is after the fish.

Send in the Hog
to shoo that Dog!

Oh my!

The Hog is eating the cake.

Sending the Hog
was a big mistake.

Send in the Cow.

Send that Cow NOW!

Oh no!

The Cow is dancing
with a mop.

Send in the Sheep
to make her stop!

Goodness!

The Sheep is tangled
in yarn.

Send in the Hen
from the barn!

Mercy!

The Hen is laying eggs
on the table.

Send in the Horse
from the stable!

Heavens!

The Horse kicked a hole
in the wall.

Send in the Elephant
to get rid of them ALL!

The Elephant was BIG,
but he squeezed through the door.

Once he was in,
there was room for no more.

Out of the house marched
the Cat and the Cow.

Out came the Horse and
the Hen and the Hog.

Out walked the Sheep.

Out ran the Dog.

But then from within,
there came a shout:

EEK! There's a Mouse in the house!